AF424405

It's Fracking Brilliant!

A Novella by Edwin Canevari
and Thomas Kuzmik

In Loving Memory of Natalie
Wood

Copyright 2020

Chapter I. The Mississippi Falls

"He don't know."

"How could he know?"

"Dat's right. He been in Solitaire fo' da last six year. Ain't no way he could know."

"Yeah, he got no way o' knowin'"

"HE" has a name. Abner Rezba. The Bastard of Bipolarity. Serving two consecutive life terms plus ninety-nine years for killing a Louisiana State Trooper, and also for killing two inmates while incarcerated in Cajun State Prison near the mouth of the Mississippi River.

It was all happening quickly now for Abner, after six years of stagnation. No human contact. Just slop on a plate sliding through the tiny door of his cell, every stinking day for over two thousand days.

He don't know. But one thing that Abner *did* know was that there were two things in the world: The

Way Things Are and The Way Things Ought To Be. And The Way Things Are always came out on top. And they always worked against Abner.

Except today.   For some mysterious and inexplicable reason, the planets today aligned differently. The flipped coin landed on its edge. The unlikeliest of unlikely was about to happen, like Donerail winning the 1913 Kentucky Derby at odds of 91 to 1.

A bad case of salmonella recently hit the regular prison guard population. A door that is always locked was inadvertently left unlocked, with keys still in the door, by one of the substitute guards. Three inmates who could never have successfully planned an escape out of a cardboard box—Heavy Jackson, Roosevelt Washington and Clarence Calhoun—were suddenly on their way out the door. And they decided to take Abner Rezba with them. Congratulations, Abner, you just won the Inmate Lottery!

Today was Victory Day for The Way Things Ought To Be. The only fly in the ointment was the thing that Abner did not know.

As Jackson and Washington and Calhoun came by to unlock the door to Abner's cell in Solitary Confinement, they only had time for two words: "Come on!"

Abner didn't ask any questions. He bolted along with the other three escapees down a labyrinth of dark hallways towards the loading dock where the police speedboat was moored. It was all happening so quickly, so surreally. Abner was the fastest of the bunch and the first to reach the speedboat. And right at that moment every possible Hell was unleashed by The Way Things Are. Gunfire erupted from eight different directions, and each of the other three men dropped like loads of bricks. With no time to talk or think, Abner dove into the speedboat and turned the key. He headed North up the Mississippi for about a quarter mile before a barrage of gunfire from Officers on both river banks forced him to turn the boat around and head South down the Mississippi.

The heavily armed Officers looked at each other in disbelief for a moment, then chimed in with a chorus of "He don't know."

"Come catch me, you flat footed fools!" Abner shouted as he headed downstream towards the mouth of the Mississippi River and the Gulf of Mexico. Finally, for once, The Way Things Ought To Be were going to have their day.

There was something else that Abner Rezba knew for sure. After two thousand days in Solitary Confinement, there was no way he was going to let them take him alive. But through no fault of his own, there was still the one big thing that "Abner don't know."

As the fully throttled speedboat reached the mouth of the Mississippi, the thing that Abner "don't know" took over and determined the course of the few remaining moments of Abner Rezba's life.

Instead of entering the welcoming waters of the Gulf of Mexico, instead of bursting joyfully into Freedom, Abner and the police speedboat were launched high into the air and Abner's last words were "Aaaaaaaaaaaaah! Aaaaaaaaaaaaaaaaaaaaaaaaaaaaaaaah!" as he hurtled over the top of the Mississippi Falls. Mississippi Falls? What the hell were the Mississippi Fal

Chapter II. The Problem

With Global Warming and the melting of the polar ice caps, most of the scientific community—and nearly everyone else—expects the water levels to rise around the globe. But the opposite is happening. Water levels are falling everywhere. How can this be?

+++++++

Evidence of the falling water levels can be seen and heard nearly every day on the news.

For example, the case of prison escapee Abner Rezba hurtling to his death over the Mississippi Falls made the National News. As he attempted to escape in a speedboat heading south down the Mississippi River towards the Gulf of Mexico, Rezba, who had been locked up in solitary confinement for six years, did not know about many things that had happened. He had been cut off from all human contact, and he had been cut off from any news of the outside world. He was unaware that the water level of the Gulf of Mexico had dropped by more than two hundred feet. He was unaware that the mouth of the Mississippi River had been turned into a giant waterfall. So when he reached the waterfall, he was shocked to find himself hurled high into the air, and he plunged to his death .

+++++++

And a week later, as the U.S.S. Truman made its way up the Gulf of Suez, the captain and crew experienced an unpleasant surprise. Under the darkness of night, the huge gray aircraft carrier inched its way along. Having more in common with a giant Univac computer than with the glorious old ships of naval history, the Truman had more computer terminals aboard than it had seamen. One such sea tech, Abner Jennings Longfellow, had a befuddled expression—a very worried look—that his commanding officer instantly observed and immediately inquired about.

"What's the problem, Longfellow? I can see that worried look upon your face."

"Sir, I believe that there is a malfunction with the depth finders. Their readings don't match the charted data, and if…"

Longfellow's response was quickly interrupted by a sharp scraping sound and a loud crash. The crew members sprang into action, scurried into position, and sounded the alarms.

"We're running aground. Mayday! Mayday!"

+++++++

And in Southern Florida, Rodrigo Rodriguez and Gonzalo Gonzalez stumbled out of the Pink Pelican dive bar shortly after last call, and they weaved their way slowly down poorly lighted Barracuda Street.

"Gonzo, do you hear that?"

"Hear what, Rodrigo?"

"There's a man calling for help."

The two amigos took a right turn in the direction of the yelling and they moved as quickly as they could towards it. They approached a streetlight that shined on a small, elongated, lime-green stucco home with a tiny front yard. Gonzo and Rodrigo stared in amazement as the left side of the tiny home appeared to be ripping loose like a page torn from a magazine As the yelling reached its peak, the left half of the home thundered quickly into a gigantic sinkhole, and it became instantly buried. The yelling was suddenly replaced by tombstone silence, and Rodrigo and Gonzalo stared at each other in dumbfounded disbelief.

The following morning the newspapers and television stations reported that local authorities had determined that the ground was too unstable to excavate, and they declared the site to be the final resting place and burial ground of the home's owner, Simon Simmons.

+++++++

The disappearance of the water from the Gulf of Mexico, from the Gulf of Suez, and from the earth below the Florida sinkhole (and the home it swallowed) are in defiance of the orderly, reliable and predictable behavior of the water in the hydrologic ecosystem that has operated in a closed and consistent manner for as long as anyone can remember or has ever recorded.

With only slight variations—ebbs and flows—caused by high tides, low tides, stormy weather and periodic droughts, the location and levels of water could be identified with mathematical precision. As the great Russian hydrologist Igor Shiklomanov explained in various detailed publications—prepared for the UNESCO International Hydrological Programme--for centuries the world's water supply was naturally renewable and selfpurifying, and water resources seemed immutable and inexhaustible.

But suddenly and inexplicably the water levels everywhere around the world are dropping dramatically, and this is happening at a time when the exact opposite is expected, with the melting of the polar ice caps due to global warming.

Expectedly, citizens of every country are reprimanded for wasting water, and they are encouraged—and in some cases legally required—to carefully limit the use of water.

But those reprimands and restrictions are only directed towards the symptoms, not the causes of The Problem. Is it up to the Experts to come up with a Solution?

Chapter III. The Bureaucrats

The esteemed members of the United Nations Committee on Global Warming listen intently as the Chairman, Jimanji Tiller, summarizes their objective and their tasks.

"Gentlemen and ladies, we are tasked to explain a most unusual and mysterious phenomenon.

With global warming and the gradual melting of the polar ice caps, it is logical to extrapolate and assume that the water levels around the globe would be rising. But the opposite is happening. Water levels around the world are falling. How can this be?

"We know from the meticulous calculations of the eminent Russian hydrologist Dr. Igor Shiklomanov that the world's water supply is constant. Of course, water is continuously metamorphosing from solid to liquid to gas, and back. And water is continuously moving via Sublimation and Desublimation, Precipitation, Groundwater Flow and Seepage, Evaporation and Evapotranspiration, Fog Drip, Plant Uptake, Absorption by Flora and Fauna, Vents and Volcanoes and Volcanic Steam. "And we also know, from the scientific consensus of the Intergovernmental Panel on Climate Change that there are expected regional differences.

Climate models, based on fundamental thermodynamics, project that Global Warming may result in higher water levels in wet zones and lower water levels in dry zones; but there are no projections that predict lower water levels in all zones.

"The question, quite simply, is '***Where is all of the water going***?'"

As the Chairman opened the floor for further discussion, the Members quickly agreed that there was a need to form a number of Committees to divide and conquer the Problem.

Committee A was formed to update and recalculate Dr. Shiklomanov's figures.

Committee B was formed to measure and track water levels in Antarctica.

Committee C was formed to measure and track water levels in the Australian/Oceania regions of Fiji and French Polynesia.

Committee D was formed to measure and track water levels in the African regions of Namibia and Niger and Nigeria.

Committee E was formed to measure and track water levels in the Asian regions of Bahamas and Bangladesh and Bhutan.

Committee F was formed to measure and track water levels in the European regions of Albania and Andorra and Armenia and Austria and Azerbaijan.

Committee G was formed to measure and track water levels in the South American regions of Bolivia and Brazil.

Committee H was formed to measure and track water levels in the North American regions of Anquilla and Antigua and Aruba.

Committee I was formed to measure and track water levels in the North American regions of Bahamas and Barbados and Belize and Bermuda.

Committee J was formed to measure and track water levels in the North American regions of Canada and Cayman and Costa Rica and Cuba.

Committee K was formed to measure and track water levels in...

Chapter IV. The NERDS

Seated in front of a giant computer screen in a dorm room at Massachusetts Institute of Technology, Bryan Hagan speaks into his televideo-linked microphone. Bryan is an All American Boy in every sense of the word: Senior Class President, Captain of the football team, both a natural leader and an elected leader.
And he is also a straight A student.

"All right, Skypers. This meeting of the Northeast Regional Doctors of Science is called to order.

"Ann Arbor, are you there, Reggie?"

"Present and accounted for. Go Blue!"

Reggie is a star tackle for the Wolverines. He looks like a big, dumb jock but in reality he has made the Dean's list during every trimester at Michigan. And there is an abbreviated version of "The Victors" sung at the Big House every time big Number 77 sacks a quarterback.

"Durham, do you read me, Hal?"

"Loud and clear! Go Blue Devils!"

Hal is a third generation computer geek with a double major in Computer Science and Paranormal Studies at Duke. He can read your C ++ code, he can read your palm, and he can read your mind.

"Palo Alto, Ravishing Rebecca?"

"Here!"

"We missed you last week, Ravishing Rebecca. How was your Natalie Wood Film Festival?"

"Yummy. Absolutely scrumptious! The Castro District in San Francisco was rockin' and rollin'. As my philosophy professor Karl Kennenbaum used to say, no Socratic Ideals have ever existed in the real world...with the exception of Natalie Wood!"

"Right on, Ravishing Rebecca. I believe. I believe. And by the way, you have a special message from a not so secret admirer in Mumbai."

"A message?"

"Yes, Rebecca. Puru sends his love. He says it is good quality of love."

"I'm flattered," Rebecca responded with an ear to ear grin that could be felt in her sultry voice.

Ravishing Rebecca Roxov is a "Cliche Girl." Not that she speaks in cliches, but that she is spoken of in cliches. Nearly everyone who meets Ravishing Rebecca says that she is "sharp as a tack" or "smart as a whip" or "cute as a button." But Ravishing Rebecca is anything but cliched in her thought patterns and emotional responses and personal devotions. She has idolized Natalie Wood for as long as she can remember. Many observers have suggested to Rebecca that, with her petite frame and piercing dark eyes and lush brunette hair, Rebecca calls to mind the great and beautiful Russian-

American actress Natalie Wood. And in fact, Rebecca has long considered Natalie Wood to be her mentor and beacon and guiding light and muse. She copies Natalie's facial expressions, voice intonations, and of course her style of walking and dressing. Rebecca consciously scurries around with quick and deliberate steps, the way that Natalie did in *Sex and the Single Girl*. She exaggerates surprise and wonder and joy and disappointment the way that Natalie did as a little girl in *Miracle on 34th Street*. She acts condescending and blasé the way that Natalie did in *This Property is Condemned*. And most of all, Rebecca is a talented seamstress who has duplicated the fabulous outfits that Natalie Wood wore in *The Great Race* and *Penelope* and *Gypsy* and many other films.

"Los Angeles. Elwood?"

There was no response from Los Angeles.

"Elwood? Elwood Buffoon?"

Reggie interjected "I heard he was arrested in

Beverly Hills."

"Arrested? What was he arrested for?"

"Suspicious behavior."

"Suspicious behavior? What suspicious behavior?"

"He was picking his nose."

"Picking his nose? What is so suspicious about that?"

"People don't pick their noses in Beverly Hills!"

Loud Out Laughter from all!

"Typical NERDY humor, you goofy Brainiacs. Let's move on to Saint Petersburg."

"Saint Petersburg. Mikhail Fyodorovich?"

Mikhail Fyodorovitch is a total Russian Nerd, brilliant in mathematics and computer science, and a fanatic about the great Russian writer,

Fyodor Dostoevsky.   He has a Dostoevsky quote for every occasion.

"Da. I am ready and willing and able."

"Berlin. Hans Jurgen?"

"Ja wol. Thy wish is mein command."

Hans Jurgen is at the top of his class at the University of Berlin, and he is also an award winning horse trainer.   His grandfather is the winningest driver in German trotting race history, and he has passed on the gift of "soft hands" to Hans Jurgen.

"London. Are you ready to roll, Rupert?"

"I bloody well am, Dr. Hagan!"

Rupert is a direct descendant of the Earl of Sandwich, and he is a purveyor of food and ale to some of London's oldest and most beloved pubs.

"Good then," Bryan continues. "Having exhausted our inquiries into the Poincare Conjecture, Fermat's Last Theorem, and the Bridges of Konigsberg, we will next be turning our attention to a problem that is presently stimying a United Nations committee, namely, the falling water levels worldwide at a time when water levels are expected to rise due to Global Warming and the melting of the polar ice caps. Or more simply stated, ***Where is the water disappearing to?***

"You probably saw on the news last week the incident with the U.S.S. Truman going aground." "The U.S.S. Truman, named in honor of our last great President, Harry S Truman!" shouted Rebecca.

"Give 'em Hell, Harry!" added Hal.

"He said that he never gave anyone Hell. All that he did was tell the truth, and to them that *was* Hell!" chimed in Reggie.

"When they were talking about Hell, do you think they had visions of fire and brimstone? A place of punishment?" inquired Hal.

"Well," piped in Mikhail, "scriptures aside, there are two basic philosophical views of Hell. The

Russian view, stated by Dostoevsky in *The
Brothers Karamazov,* is that Hell is the suffering of
being unable to love. But the
French view, stated by Sartre in *No Exit,* is that
Hell is OTHER PEOPLE!"

"Especially NERDS!" laughed Ravishing Rebecca.

"Leave it to the Frenchmen!" smirked
Hal. "They even take a negative view of
positive ions!"

"And when they play Johnny Mercer, they change
his classic tune to AC-CENT-TCHU-
ATE THE NEGATIVE!"

"Oh my," gasped Hans Jurgen. "The Russians have
Marshal Suvorov, who never lost a battle. But the
French have General DeGaulle, who never WON a
battle!"

Laughing Out Loud all around!

"LOL!" screamed Reggie. "LOL!" shouted Hal.

"By the way, speaking of Harry S Truman. What did the S stand for?" asked Mikhail. "SIR, of course!" responded Rupert.

"I thought it was 'Sampson' the Biblical strongman," chimed in Reggie.

"Or maybe it was just plain 'Strength' added Rebecca.

"And by the way, this problem of the Disappearing Water will undoubtedly be our biggest problem ever!" exclaimed Reggie.

"Not necessarily. We may be facing an even bigger and more dangerous problem" interjected Mikhail Fyodorovitch.

"What problem is that, Mikhail?" inquired Bryan?

"The Thunder of Allah!" replied Mikhail Fyodorovitch.

"The Thunder of Allah? What is the Thunder of Allah?" inquired Rupert.

Chapter V. The Mad Professor's Wild Hot Lava Ride

The Mad Professor, Justin Bold, had predicted to his students, followers, minions and devotees that the next eruption of the world's most active volcano, Kilauea in Hawaii, was going to be something special and unforgettable and different from anything anyone anywhere had ever seen before.

Kilauea had been erupting and spewing, on and off, for the past thirty five years. But now Pele, the goddess of fire and lightning and wind and volcanoes, was applying intense pressure to the Pacific Tectonic Plate.

There has been a long standing tradition of good luck and blessings when lovers and love makers attempted to sync up their love, and their love making, with the inextinguishable, natural power of volcanic nature. They covered the hillsides surrounding the mighty volcano with wool blankets and bamboo mats, and especially family heir loom Hawaiian throw blankets.

The lovers attempted to get on same wavelength as Haumea, the Havaiian goddess of fertility, and they attempted to time their personal orgasms with Kilauea's eruption.

The most blessed and fortunate among them timed their greatest, most intense moment of sexual love with the blast of Kilauea's eruption. In essence, they experienced a simultaneous orgasm with Mother Earth!

Thousands of lovers and love makers, young and old, married and single, rich and poor, lined the hills and lava beds with their own beds, feverishly sharing their natural rhythms with the Earth's rhythm, in an orgiastic festival of blessed natural love. Their moans and groans and deeply ecstatic cries of sexual joy were amplified into shouts and screams of deeply devotional prayer at the moment of Kilauea's volcanic eruption.

The devotees and votaries arrived days, weeks, and sometimes even months in advance of the Holy Mountain's anticipated release of smoke and cinders and ash and hot lava.

Because of Mad Professor Justin Bold's prediction and promise of something new and exciting and totally different and unexpected, the crowd was much, much larger than usual.

As the rumbling and grumbling of Mighty Kilauea grew louder and more intense, the collective lovemaking grew more frantic and indulgent, and tender caring gave way to reckless abandon. And the vibrating and gyrating and pulsating reached a fever pitch. Most, of course, lost control, could not contain their own personal eruptions, and gave way seconds or minutes or hours before Kilauea let loose with her powerful roaring blast. After reaching orgasm, most of the lovers and love makers quietly and comfortably settled into gentle caresses of the "spoons position" and many slowly and gradually entered the special and mysterious zone of Rapid Eye Movement sleep.

When the long awaited and triumphant release of Kilauea herself finally arrived, only a blessed handful shouted out in perfect harmony with the Ancient Mother of Volcanic Energy. The screams of those few, however, were so intense and mystical and loving and filled with such immeasurable pure energy that they awakened even those who had dozed off.

But this year there truly was something special, something magical, something bizarre, a unique moment worthy of the Great Showman P.T. Barnum. As Kilauea erupted, hot gases and smoke and luminescent fiery red lava exploded out, but they were accompanied by an unexpected, louder than ever, scream of electronic joy.

A brightly lighted sphere was suddenly ejected by Kilauea in a perfect parabolic arc, accompanied by a deafening scream over a super modified police blowhorn.

"Yeeeeeeeeeeeeeeeeeeeeeee Haaaaaaaaaaaaaaaaaaaa!!!!!!!!!

Chooooooooooooooooooooooo Eeeeeeeeeeeeeeeeeeeeeeeeee Baby!!!!" boomed the voice of the Mad Professor, Justin Bold.

The gathered revelers and worshippers watched with delight as a Titanium Sphere, at the end of the parabolic trip, landed in the middle of the glowing red river of molten lava. Stabilized in the river of lava, the lid of the sphere popped open, and the sphere's passenger stood up. The crowd of revelers and lovers and love makers clapped and applauded and screamed and shouted praise for the incredible Mad Professor Justin Bold as the remarkable titanium tub travelled down the flowing lava river on its journey to the sea.

Thus, at this magic moment, the Mad Professor's Wild Hot Lava Ride became the fulfillment of Mad Professor Justin Bold's Lifetime Dream—a history making trip in a Titanium Tub down Kilauea's River of Molten Lava. Snapping pictures and recording video along the way, Professor Bold also used his mind boggling array of complex instruments to record and measure this special event in scientific history.

Smiling and waving and gesticulating to the crowd, Professor Bold looked like a foreign dignitary on a triumphant procession. And triumphant it truly was. And at the end of the Titanium Tub's journey, as the red hot lava dumped into the cool ocean water, Professor Bold temporarily disappeared into a giant erupting cloud of SIZZLING STEAM.

And the almost unimaginable power of the volcano, and the intense heat and energy bottled up within the Earth's core, was going to play a key and essential role in the effort to solve the problem of the world's disappearing waters.

Chapter VI. The Thunder of Allah

"What exactly is the Thunder of Allah?" asked Rupert.

"More precisely, WHO is the Thunder of Allah?" responded Mikhail Fyodorovich. "Our contacts at the University of Cairo have been reporting rumors about the Thunder of Allah for months now, but just this week we received some important confirmations.

"Here is a summary of their findings. Even the most devastating forest fire can start with a single spark. Such has been the impact of the Thunder of Allah, a mysterious and shadowy figure rumored about, through all of the Arab World, although it is difficult to find anyone who actually knows, or has even met, the Thunder of Allah.

It all began with whispers in the desert, talks about the way things are, and talks about the way things ought to be. What began as mere conjecture has erupted with volcanic intensity and is now accepted as undisputed truth. It has fueled a movement larger and more powerful than anything ever before seen in the Arab World. And we are only now beginning to hear much about it in the Western World. Sunnis and Shiites, Saudis and Syrians and Iraquis, Nomads and City Dwellers all speak of the Thunder of Allah with enthusiasm and reverence, and many view him as a prophet and emissary sent directly by Muhammad.

"And after all, it makes such perfect sense. The widespread perception is that, in everything it says and everything it does, the Infidel World is out to destroy the Arab World. Disputes about oil are serious and continual, and fortunes rise and fall with each attack on and counterattack from the oil producing Mideast. And although

Oil has undeniable importance, Water is *Life Itself!*

"And it does not take much arm twisting to convince the Arab World that the Americans, the Russians, or both, are plotting to destroy Arabia by forming a Water Cartel that will control the world's water supply and then restrict, and ultimately eliminate Arab access to precious, life sustaining water.

"So where do we start?" asked the disciplined and methodical Hans Jurgen?

I say we should start with our own private Mata Hari-- Ravishing Rebecca," Bryan suggested. "If she puts on her seductive black dress, the copy of the dress worn by Natalie Wood in *The Great Race,* Ravishing Rebecca will no doubt be loosening lips and sinking ships." Bryan was referring to the dresses that Rebecca had duplicated with her seamstress skills, imitations of famous outfits that Natalie Wood had worn throughout her career. The hoop skirt and bright red coat from *Rebel Without*

A Cause, the black dress from *The Great Race,* the low cut number from *This Property Is Condemned,* the electric blue form-fitting stunner from *Gypsy,* the bikinis and the pink bra—immortalized and housed in the Frederick's of Hollywood Museum— that Natalie wore in *Bob and Carol and Ted and Alice.*

"Any objections, Rebecca?" inquired Hal.

"None whatsoever," responded Ravishing Rebecca. "I will be happy to take the lead on the Thunder of Allah fact finding mission."

"And Hal," Bryan inquired, "Will you take the lead on the problem of the disappearing water?" "My pleasure, Bryan," Hal responded.

"Where will you start, Rebecca?" inquired Rupert.

"Well, Rupert, I happen to know that the Arab Studies Department is holding an Open House this Friday, and if I pull out my replica of Natalie's red coat from *Rebel Without A Cause,* and put on those classic bright red lips, I may be able to get the ball rolling.

"I believe, I believe" repeated Bryan, those beloved and memorable words uttered by little Natalie in *Miracle on 34th Street.*

"And where will you start, Hal?" asked Rupert.

"I know just what you're thinking, Rupert," responded Hal. "And you're right. I'm going to dig up our old research on the Canals of Mars, and I'm going to pull Professor Shiklomanov's papers on the World's Water Supply."

Then, with the enthusiasm of a Durham Bulls fan keeping a scorecard, Hal started to jot down his initial task and "to do" list. And with enough faith to move mountains, Ravishing Rebecca began her quest to discover the Thunder of Allah.

+++++++

Ravishing Rebecca brought her *"A Game"* of charm to the Arab Studies Open House.

She was decked out in her replica bright red coat that Natalie Wood wore in *Rebel Without A Cause,* and lips adorned in Maybelline blazing red lipstick. And beneath her bright red coat, Rebecca wore the stunning black dress that looked like Natalie's little black dress in *The Great Race*. She was ready to loosen lips and sink ships, and she was indeed the hit of the Open House.

Every man turned his head when Rebecca entered the Open House Ballroom, with her stunning outfit, her blazing red lips, and the beguiling scent of Jungle Gardenia, Natalie's favorite perfume. The visiting Arab dignitaries, especially, took note of this irresistible young lady, and her dance card filled up quickly.

Rebecca's first dance was with the emissary Ali El Amin, and she flirted playfully with him as she tried to learn something about the Thunder of Allah.

"Ah, the Thunder of Allah" explained Ali El Amin, "No, that is not really a person. It is a personification of thoughts and ideas, concepts and trusted beliefs. No, you will never meet him, because he does not exist."

Rebecca's next dance was with the diplomat Abdullah Nejem. Rebecca waltzed expertly and precisely with Nejem, and she gazed lovingly into his eyes in an effort to soften him up.

"No, there is no one who has met the man Thunder of Allah, because that is just a phrase like 'Hand of God' or 'Providence.' It is a convenient expression, not a living being."

Rebecca's third dance was with the scholar Ahmad El Hashem. Rebecca used all of her charm to try to pry some valuable information from the learned academic. She moved her shoulders like Natalie did in *Sex and the Single Girl*, she strutted like Natalie in *Gypsy*, and she even made reference to a friend of hers who had spoken with Thunder of Allah.

"Oh, Thunder of Allah is not one man, but many men. He is an adopted name, of sorts, like the name 'Kilroy' that your American soldiers used in World War II to commemorate their presence throughout Europe when they wrote 'Kilroy was here.'"

Rebecca's fourth dance was with the salesman Hakim Samara. Rebecca mentioned to Samara that the Thunder of Allah must be very well traveled because he has been mentioned in so many different places.

"No, my dear. The Thunder of Allah is nothing more than a marketing gimmick, much like your New Englanders use 'George Washington slept here.' If George Washington really slept in all of those places, he would have to change his name to Rip Van Winkle!"

Rebecca's fifth dance was with ombudsman Zaman Tawfeek. Rebecca prevaricated, and told Tawfeek that she heard that Tawfeek had dined with Thunder of Allah a week ago, and she wondered if they had discussed anything interesting.

"Oh my dear, you have misunderstood. I did not dine *with* Thunder of Allah, last week. I dined *upon* Thunder of Allah. You see, Thunder of Allah is a marvelous Kurdish dish that is a variation of biraska sise, like Russian shashlik, but with added touches of fruits to the traditional meat and vegetable kabob. It is all the rage right now in the Arab world."

As sharp and insightful and perceptive as Ravishing Rebecca was, even she could not tell if these Arab dignitaries were being evasive, or if they were honestly ignorant of the existence and identity of the Thunder of Allah. But for now, she felt that she was "barking up the wrong tree," and she would have to use a different approach to make contact with the Thunder of Allah.

Ravishing Rebecca Roxov turned to the Internet. She started tracking blogs and discussion groups, and she touched base with some journalism students to see if they could monitor *Al Jazeera* newscasts for information related to the Thunder of Allah. And she conferred with Mikhail to check out some of the facts that he had compiled.

"You know, Rebecca, as Dostoevsky's protege Nietzsche used to say, 'There are no facts, only *interpretations of facts!'*"

"You're not helping, Mikhail!" Rebecca lamented.

Meanwhile, Hal was scouring their old research about the Canals of Mars, Reggie was studying Professor Shiklomanov's papers on the World's Water Supply, and Bryan was reading the latest publications on underground water detection.

Chapter VII. The Brink

For thousands of years, humans have talked about and predicted the end of the world.

Famous examples include:

- Assyrian Tablets in 2800 B.C. stated that "the end of the world is evidently approaching"

- Early Christians in 1st Century A.D believed that the world would end "any day now"

- Hilary of Poitiers predicted the end of the world in 365 A.D.

- 7th Century Muslims believed that the Qiyamah (Last Judgment) was imminent

- Hippolytus of Rome, around 200 A.D., predicted that the world would end in 500 A.D.

- Pope Sylvester II, in 999 A.D., said the world would end in 1000 A.D. (Millennium Apocalypse)

- In 1562 Nostradamus prophesied that the King of Terror would end the world in 1999

- Martin Luther predicted the world would end by 1600 A.D.

- In 1501 Christopher Columbus predicted the world would end in 1656

- The Shakers believed the world would end in 1794

- John Wesley foresaw that the world would end in 1836

- Herbert W. Amrstrong predicted "end world" in 1936 then 1943 then 1972 then 1975

But for the first time in human history, and from a genuine scientific viewpoint, Apocalypse and Armageddon truly seemed possible.

Global pollution had reached such dense and dangerous levels that now—to the sorrow and grief of scientists and lay people alike—even the once pristine polar ice caps show indications of excessive lead and other metals.

Global warming—still a matter of dispute and controversy and varying interpretation—revived deep seated fears when meteorologists announced that July, 2015, was the hottest July in the recorded weather history dating back to the 1880's.

Global overpopulation has been a source of steadily growing concern, exacerbated by Pope Paul VI's birth control encyclical *Humanae Vitae*. Fears about maintaining the food supply have been surpassed recently by heightening fears about an inability to maintain the world's water supply, calculated by Professor Igor Shiklomanov as a daily need of 40 gallons per person per day.

And the imminent threat of Nuclear devastation and annihilation increased as the Nuclear Agreement with Iran was hashed and rehashed and re-rehashed, as North Korea triggered test after test after test, and as rumors spread about a new and unthinkably terrible weapon of destruction, a hand held Nuclear grenade.

+++++++

As Mikhail loved to point out, in *Notes from Underground,* Dostoevsky divided humans into two categories: people of consciousness and people of action. And the United Nations, as usual, consisted of many people of consciousness and very few people of action. The vast majority of the members and delegates and representatives were too wrapped up in political correctness to see the vital issues clearly and, hence, were unable to attack the problems head on.

So the U.N. Committees and Delegations were filled with a sense of bewilderment regarding the speed with which the gatherings and demonstrations spread, and the violent rate at which the size of the protesting crowds grew.

Chapter VIII. The Riots

Two weeks ago a furious crowd of 50,000 gathered in The Casbah in Algiers to protest against the West for attempting to form a Water Cartel. Angry Arabs shouted, screamed, and then raised their clenched fists as they vowed severe and violent retaliation against Western attempts to cut off the Arab world from precious, life maintaining water.

A week later 150,000 protesters in Beirut's Martyrs Square had to be dispersed by fire hoses and police batons.

Four days after that a crowd of 500,000 in Cairo's Tahrir Square burned effigies of Western leaders.

And three days later an out of control crowd of 1,000,000 stormed Bahrat Square in Damascus and ran wildly, swinging machetes and chanting metaphysical threats of death and eternal damnation. And thousands of imitation Western Heads were chopped off and sent rolling through the streets.

And the Arab Fury was raging out of control.

Western National leaders were burned in effigy. Flags and symbols were trampled and stomped into obliteration. Mock firing squads performed executions, and thousands of imitation western heads were chopped off and rolling.

And those were just the visible signs. Spreading even more quickly and growing even more rapidly were the secret and underground retaliatory groups who plotted against the water supplies of the Western World.

Groups that monitor Internet activity reported a logarithmic jump in the number of Internet downloads of the schematics of the world's dams, reservoirs, and water distribution systems. And, of course, a sharp increase in the ever present inquiries about how to obtain the radioactive ingredients for the most coveted of recipes--a nuclear weapon of mass destruction.

In the United States, Stage 5 Red Alerts were issued for every strategic water site from Niagara Falls to the Hoover Dam, and Homeland Security doubled and tripled the monitoring of every Internet

Protocol Address downloading schematics, and every email containing reference to water.

In Canada, the Royal Canadian Mounted Police were assigned emergency duty to keep watch over the Daniel Johnson Dam on the Manicouagan River, the W.A.C. Bennett Dam on the Peace River, and the Robert Bourasa Dam on the La Grande River.

In Russia, one hundred troops were assigned to day and night patrol of the Zeya Dam on the Zeya River and the Krasnoyarsk Dam on the Yenisey River; and two hundred troops were assigned around the clock to safeguard the Bratsk Dam on the Angara River.

And the United States and Canada and Russia, as well as the majority of the Euro and ANZAC countries and territories, placed a thirty day moratorium on all immigration activity. They were buying time, and they were all instituting security measures just short of martial law.

Chapter IX. The Lady

The End of the World became more likely with each passing day. The Northeast Regional Doctors of Science had stretched their tentacles into every conceivable academic field and into even the remotest universities and academic centers on Earth. They brilliantly included hydrologists, volcanologists, biologists, oceanographers, physicists, chemists, astronomers, seismologists, meteorologists, ecologists...and last but not least, fracking technologists.

Inspired initially by the Canals of Mars, and the persistent mystery of "Why does Mars have Canals with no water in them?" the NERDS followed an inevitable chain of logic. The absence of water in the Canals of Mars has two logical explanations:

1. The water evaporated into the atmosphere
2. The water sank deeper inside the planet

Applying that logic to the disappearance of the water from the Earth's ecosystem, the NERDS eliminated the first possibility because, since recording of the data had begun over one hundred years ago, there was no measurable change in the humidity- globally- of the Earth's atmosphere.

So the only real possibility was that the water was not exactly "disappearing" but rather "relocating" somewhere beneath the Earth's surface. And after all, Urban Studies had for years identified water collecting in huge underground caverns beneath cities like Chicago and New York from which millions of gallons of water had to be pumped out daily.

Despite the natural relocation of water due to earthquakes, volcanoes, hurricanes, etc, there was one glaring and relatively recent "unnatural act" that was being committed on a daily basis and which was realigning the Water Table— FRACKING!

By fracturing the natural barrier of bedrock, and by loosening the water retentive power of both clay and sandy soil, the Frackers were releasing hidden stores of valuable gas and oil; but they were also creating caves and caverns into which precious water could, and did, flow and accumulate. And the

Frackers also gravelized the formerly solid rock layer that became absorbent and capable of retaining megatons and megatons of water.

Having identified the caves and caverns into which water had sunk and accumulated, and the gravelized rock that had soaked up additional water, the NERDS had to answer one final question: How can the disappeared/relocated water be reclaimed and brought back into the Earth's eco water system?

The answer had been provided to Mikhail Fyodorovitch by the eminent, the inevitable, the improbable Mad Professor Justin Bold. "The water can be heated and changed from a liquid to a gas, which will rise to the surface" postulated Mikhail Fyodorovitch.

"Heated with what?" asked Hans Jurgen?

"Volcanic heat."

"But there are only around a thousand volcanoes in the world."

"Yes, but as Professor Bold pointed out, if you count Volcanic Fields, Conder Caves, Maars, Magma Chambers and Individual Eruptions Centers, the number is much higher."

"How much higher?"

"Nobody has ever counted all of them—but probably MILLIONS!"

"So some of the errant water can be retrieved by volcanically heating the liquid into a gas which rises to the surface. But how about the water trapped in caves, and in galvanized rocks?"

"Ravishing Rebecca, do you care to answer that question?"

"That water," Ravishing Rebecca responded, "can be accumulated with natural and genetically engineered artificial sponges."

"And how can it be brought back to the surface?" challenged Hans Jurgen?

"By the roots of the Super Bamboo Fig tree."

"The Super What?"

"The Super Bamboo Fig tree. It is a hybrid developed at the University of Sydney. It is a cross between the fastest growing plant— bamboo--and the tree with the deepest growing roots, the South African wild fig. In semi-weightless hydroponic tanks, the Bamboo Fig has grown at a rate of three feet per day, and the roots have grown to nearly a thousand feet." Now that the challenging scientific portion of the solution had been worked out, the most difficult task remained: how could the NERDS reach the Thunder of Allah to present their facts, persuade him that there was **not** a conspiratorial plot by The West to deprive Arabia of precious water, and convince him to calm down the raging tempers in the Arab World; and, ultimately, enlist his help in implementing "The Solution" first in the Arab world, and then step by step throughout the rest of the water dependent world.

Ravishing Rebecca had attended Open Houses, monitored classes, listened to lectures, perused articles, and commissioned translations of newpapers and magazines and transcripts of radio and television broadcasts, but all of her efforts arrived at similar dead ends.

But leave it to social butterfly Ravishing Rebecca to finally figure out how to reach the Thunder of Allah. She had read "Six Degrees of Separation" and had determined that she personally was only two degrees of separation from the President of the United States, and only three degrees of separation from the Pope. Rebecca took it on faith that she was no more than six degrees of separation from the Thunder of Allah. The difficult part was identifying who he was. But then a light went on for Ravishing Rebecca. It was not necessary to determine his identity. It was only necessary to identify the "Chain of Six" that would connect her to the Thunder of Allah and make it possible to communicate the NERDS' urgent message.

Ravishing Rebecca knew a guy who knew a gal who knew the admissions director at the University of Arabia. That admissions director, in turn, knew the admissions directors of all of the universities in the Arab World, and somewhere in that mix there had to be SOMEONE who knew how to communicate with the Thunder of Allah, how to "send a message" to him.

So Ravishing Rebecca sent out an urgent "Mayday" of her own to all of her contacts, the contacts of her contacts, and the contacts of the contacts of her contacts.

And sure enough, within three days Ravishing Rebecca was put in touch with someone who knew—but refused to reveal the name or identify of—the Thunder of Allah. Ravishing Rebecca referred to her source as "Shallow Throat" and she began a patient but urgent process of transferring bits and pieces of critical information (but no money) to Shallow Throat, with the hope that Shallow Throat would have the sense and conscience to pass the information on to the Thunder of Allah.

In general, the NERDS felt that it was a long shot (or as Reggie would say, "a chance between slim and none") that 1) The information would ever reach the Thunder of Allah or 2) Even if the information reached the Thunder of Allah, that he would believe it, much less respond favorably to it.

But miracles sometimes happen, and not only on 34th Street. Within two days, Shallow Throat contacted Ravishing Rebecca—to the shock and surprise of the rest of the NERDS—with news that the Thunder of Allah was "intrigued" by the data.

The Thunder of Allah agreed to meet with Ravishing Rebecca and several other NERDS, but the meeting had to take place at Shangri La—the Center for Islamic Arts and Cultures in Hawaii. Shangri La was a place of peace and wisdom. It had been built by the famous heiress and philanthropist Doris Duke, who had been known simply as "The Lady" by the citizens of Newport, Rhode Island, when she resided there. When heiress Doris Duke (the world's richest woman and the daughter of tobacconist James Buchanan Duke) married James Cromwell in 1935, they embarked on a year long honeymoon that was tantamount to a world tour. The couple traveled extensively throughout Egypt, India, Indonesia, China and Japan. During her honeymoon, Doris Duke became fascinated with

Islamic Art and Culture. The last stop on the honeymoon was Hawaii, and it was there that Doris Duke decided to build a home (later to become a museum) devoted to Islamic Architecture and Art and Culture. She named her home Shangri La, after the mystical, harmonious valley in James Hilton's 1933 novel *Lost Horizon*. In the novel, Shangri La was an earthly paradise, a mythical utopia in the Himalaya mountains, and an eternally joyful place that was safe from the outside world. And this is what Doris Duke envisioned for her Hawaiian Shangri La.

Three years after their honeymoon, Doris Duke and James Cromwell returned to the Middle East to acquire works of art for Shangri La from historic and ancient cities such as Alexandria, Baghdad, Cairo, Damascus, Istanbul and Teheran. And the collection continued to grow for the next sixty years. With an approach of "inventive synthesis," the collection mixing original and commissioned pieces grew to more than several thousand works.

So it was here, in this historic place of peace and culture, that the meeting with the NERDS and the Thunder of Allah was destined to take place.

Ravishing Rebecca could not help but reflect on the similar life experiences of heiress Doris Duke and Rebecca's idol, actress Natalie Wood. Both had a difficult time trusting anyone because, time after time, individuals who seemed interested in them as people, in becoming their trusted friends and confidantes and even their spouses, inevitably turned out to only be opportunists and gold diggers who wanted Doris's or Natalie's fortunes to spend, or Doris's or Natalie's fame to boost their own careers and influence.

When Ravishing Rebecca responded with a confirmation of the meeting at Shangri La, Shallow Throat provided another surprise. Still without revealing the true identify of the Thunder of Allah, Shallow Throat revealed a smattering of biographical facts.

The Thunder of Allah was born in the city of Al Ain in the United Arab Emirates. Al Ain meant "The

Spring" in Arabic, and it was a miraculous city that sprang up (pun intended) in the middle of the desert because of the surprising water source. The Thunder of Allah was well educated, and he even—to Rupert's shock and disbelief—spent some time at the prestigious University of London. Shallow Throat described the terms of the meeting, which were clear and simple.

The Thunder of Allah would bring an entourage of twelve associates. And Ravishing Rebecca would be allowed to bring six associates. Oddly enough, there were seven NERDS in total, and exactly seven NERDS were allowed to attend. Had the Thunder of Allah also been doing his homework?

If there was any sign of bureaucratic or law enforcement presence, the meeting would be immediately and ferociously canceled, and any future attempts at discussions or negotiations would be fruitless and pointless.

These were the terms: take them of leave them. And of course Ravishing Rebecca took them, and ran with them. She went to work on arranging the meeting at Shangri La. She also delegated to the other NERDS the tasks of conducting the exhaustive research on what to say, what to do, and what sort of gift to bring for the Thunder of Allah.

+++++++

On the appointed day, promptly at sunrise, the Thunder of Allah's twelve man Entourage arrived. As they approached the meeting site, they were welcomed by a lavish leather box, placed on an ivory stand. The leather box was midnight black, about five feet long, and when opened it revealed red velvet lining that housed the gift for the Thunder of Allah. It was a magnificent hand crafted and brightly gleaming double edged silver sword with a beautiful gold horse's head emblazoned on the handle. By the reaction of the twelve man Entourage, it was clear that the meeting was off to a good start. Then mysteriously, magically, as if appearing from thin air, the Thunder of Allah was majestically standing before the leather box containing the double edged sword. To Ravishing Rebecca this swarthy, bearded man dressed in a spotless, flowing white gown looked more like a vision of Jesus Christ than a raging organizer intent on destroying the Western World. And he seemed completely calm, except for a slight visible reaction when his eyes beheld Ravishing Rebecca Roxov in the stunning brimmed white hat and beautiful white dress modeled after Natalie Wood's outfit at the end of *Splendor In The Grass.*

"Sidi, Janab, Excellent Sir," began Ravishing Rebecca, "Thank you for honoring us with this meeting, and we truly hope that this gift pleases you. We call this sword "The Lady" in honor of the great philanthropist Doris Duke who was known as "The Lady"and who is responsible for the construction of this wonderful Center for Islamic Arts and Cultures. Like every lady, "The Lady" has two edges. Unlike your single edged scimitars and machetes, this blade represents and embodies the mystery and subtlety of woman, and the inscrutability of the events which, when divided and assembled, we call History.

"The great Greek philosopher Aristotle wrote that "We fight wars that we may live in peace."

"With the double edge of that paradox in mind, we genuinely hope and believe that, although we may not ever completely settle or reconcile our differences, we may nevertheless be able to reach enough common ground that we can establish a state of peaceful coexistence. In our minds, it might be thought of as a Peaceful Coexistence Coalition." The Thunder of Allah stood silent for a moment, reflected seriously, and then solemnly began to speak in a deep but soft voice.

"Thank you, gentle lady, for this marvelous gift, with its hidden meaning, and the honor it pays to its namesake, The Lady Doris Duke. I will tell you up front that, like all Arabs, the most popular phrase we accept from your culture is the esteemed Kipling's declaration that 'East is East, and West is West, and never the twain shall meet.' Politically and religiously, we do not trust your culture, your way of life. But like my Father and my Grandfather and my Great Grandfather before me, I am first and foremost a Scientist. And I am willing to review any scientific evidence you may have that will support your claims about the world's water supply.
"

And with those formalities out of the way, the scientific portion of the meeting was about to begin.

But first, because Ravishing Rebecca was well acquainted with the importance of "ice breakers," there was some prerequisite entertainment and feasting.

As the group gazed out upon the beautiful Pacific Ocean, a group of caretakers expertly walked twenty magnificent horses up to the meeting place.

"Before undertaking the difficult task before us, let us first relax with a leisurely ride along the beach. Kind sir, here comes your mount," Rebecca declared, as the most magnificent and beautiful steed was led up for the Thunder of Allah to ride.

Hans Jurgen the horseman had done an excellent job of choosing the twenty beautiful equines that would set the tone for the important, perhaps world saving, meeting ahead.

All twenty of the meeting participants mounted up and headed down towards the sandy beach. The gentle Pacific breeze refreshed them all, and the powerful horses invigorated the riders with the spirit that had been passed down for centuries through these amazing, almost mythical, creatures.

At one point, the Thunder of Allah directed his majestic stallion into the ocean water, and soon everyone else followed. It was a wondrous and happy site to see all twenty on horseback frolicking and splashing through the waves and salt water.

Feeling reborn by the wind and the breeze and the lovely sunrise, the riders headed back to Shangri La for another wonderful surprise. Rupert--with his culinary expertise that had been passed down from his ancestor the Earl of Sandwich—had arranged for a wonderful brunch consisting of American, British, Russian, German and Arabic delicacies. A team of world class chefs had been commissioned to prepare an arrangement and assortment of delicious foods that amounted not only to a feast, but also a feast for the eyes. Mangoes and peaches and figs and dates, brightly colored tomatoes and eggplants and turnips and carrots, tournedos of beef, lamb shashlik, chateaubriand and prime rib and swordfish steaks and lobster, provided something to satisfy every taste.

When the mouthwatering and delectable feast was finished, the group sat down for a moment to enjoy the view and the breeze and the harmonious and rhythmic sound of the Pacific waves. Then it was time for the agenda at hand.

Ravishing Rebecca and the other six NERDS with her brought out a thick document filled with essays and formulas and charts and graphs and photos to explain and support their thesis. And all of this heavy documentation was accompanied by a brightly colored slideshow.

The Thunder of Allah observed with respect and amazement as Ravishing Rebecca and the NERDS professionally and passionately presented their thesis with references to Igor Shiklomanov's calculations of the world's water supply, theories about the canals on the planet Mars, where the Martian canal water disappeared to, and everyday examples of vast caverns under the cities of Chicago and New York from which millions of gallons of water have to be pumped daily.

Along with the scientific facts and evidence, special tribute was paid to the insights of The Lady Doris Duke who-- when she was the wealthiest woman in the world--had discovered that wealth and resources alone could not solve every problem. Genuine Solutions depended on and required goodwill among people, kindness, generosity, wisdom, and a spirit of teamwork and cooperation in pursuit of a common goal.

Several hours later, when the presentation was completed, and the Thunder of Allah was satisfied enough by the scientific facts to at least temporarily suspend his mistrust of the Western World, Ravishing Rebecca and the other six NERDS dropped to their knees, bowed their heads, and humbly asked the Thunder of Allah for his help.

Impressed by their humility and their sincerity, the Thunder of Allah asked a simple question:
"What help do you need from me?"

And with that simple question, there opened the floodgates of The Solution to The Problem that initially seemed unsolvable because it consisted of paradox and contradiction and defiance of common sense. But in the end it was a Solution that was so

" extraordinary that it could only be described one way-- *It's Fracking Brilliant!*

Chapter X. The Solution—It's Fracking Brilliant!

"Sidi, Jahab, Esteemed Sir, the help that we ask is once again double edged, like The Lady.

"First, whatever can be done to persuade your people that maybe, just maybe, we are all in this together, and that our differences right now are not as important as our common goal—human survival through the availability of pure, clean water.

"Second, using the scientific approach that will make pure, clean water more readily available, we would like to propose that the plan begin in your part of the world.

"Unlike the double edged sword, our scientific solution is three-pronged, like Neptune's trident, or Islam's three sacred texts: Koran, Sira and Hadith And by applying some of the principles of fracking technology, hydrology, hybrids, hydroponics, geology, oceanography, physics, chemistry, biology and volcanology, what we are asking your help with is participation by your people.

"As you know, the Jews have their Star of David and the Christians have the Cross of Christ. But the symbol of your people is the Crescent, and we would like to honor your people by shaping the initial project in the form of a giant Crescent—perhaps like the Fertile Crescent in your section of the World. The Crescent is reserved for the special third part of the Solution. The first part of the Solution consists of Super Hybrid Sponges that can be located deep in the earth, in the caverns and bedrocks and gravelized and fragmented rock, so that the errant water can be soaked up for reclamation. The second part consists of Super Hybrid Bamboo Figs that grow quickly (like the bamboo) and plunge roots deeply (like the fig) to reach the sponges and draw the water back up to the surface to feed the water ecosystem.

"But the third part of the Solution, reserved for your Crescent, is based on a revision of the eminent Dr. Shiklomanov's World Water Inventory.

"The great Dr. Shiklomanov's calculations are based on the assumption that the human "usable" water supply was in Rivers and fresh water Lakes.

But the Earth is 80% water, while the Rivers and fresh water Lakes comprise only about 2% of the Earth's total water supply. It is a great irony that cities like San Diego, California, sit on the shore of the world's largest body of water, the Pacific Ocean, and yet they depend on the Colorado River for their water.

"And while the Super Hybrid Sponges and Super Hybrid Bamboo Figs can reclaim the water lost because of Fracking, the third part of the Solution can create **a brand new, and much larger, source of pure, clean water.**

"We know that there are only about a thousand volcanoes in the world. But if we count Volcanic Fields, Conder Caves, Maars, Magma Chambers and Individual Eruptions Centers, there are probably over a million sources that can heat salt water, boil and vaporize it, and send it to the surface as clean, pure Artesian spring water.

"The idea is to use fracking technology to utilize the great unused bodies of salt water. And we will start by building a Crescent shaped series of pipe feeds that will utilize gravity and volcanic heat to vaporize the water to make it fresh and pure and clean and usable.

The basic idea is that Fracking Drills can penetrate a couple of miles deep. And we know that gravity will pull water through a pipe if the angle of descent is an eighth of an inch per foot, which is an inch per eight feet, which is also a foot per every 96 feet— or nearly 100 feet horizontally for every foot vertically. Using that ratio, we can determine that gravity will pull water about 200 miles horizontally for every 2 miles vertically. We will build a Crescent shaped series of feed pipes that will extend 200 miles in many directions, and the water will be steered towards volcanic heat sources that will boil the water and send it towards the surface in wonderful Artesian springs.

"Like Al Ain," observed the Thunder of Allah.

"Exactly, Esteemed Sir!" declared Ravishing Rebecca.

The meeting then grew silent for a few moments. The silence, though, was not awkward or creepy, like in a Hitchcock movie. Rather, it was a peaceful silence, a refreshing silence, like the stillness before a beautiful sunrise.

Then the Thunder of Allah began to speak with passion and wisdom and sincerity.

"The world is in a state of War. Our world, Your world, and Everyone's world. Defense and Military and Security are big business. Attacks and Counterattacks are the order of the day. And all of this War planning and Security planning breed a deep sense of fear and mistrust. And yet, as your great actor and philanthropist Paul Newman once observed, the world cannot run without trust.

Without at least a minimal foundation of trust, there can be only Chaos.

"I commend you on your excellent presentation of your findings, and on your thesis worthy of the most brilliant doctoral candidates. And I thank you for you gift of the beautiful doubleedged sword which can serve as not only a weapon of war, but also as an instrumental preserver of peace.

I cannot promise you that all, or even many, can be persuaded that your findings are correct and accurate. I can only promise that I will do my best to disseminate your findings, to let the facts speak for themselves, and to attempt to at least create a chance for a climate of peaceful cooperation and coexistence. Like the seven of you, and like your beloved idol Natalie Wood (Ravishing Rebecca started a bit, at the mention of Natalie's name. How did he know?), I too believe in miracles. Let us hope that we are now in the midst of one of the greatest miracles of all."

As the renowned Canadian educator and hierarchiologist—and formulator of the Peter Principle-Laurence J. Peter once exclaimed, "Don't believe in miracles—depend on them!"

And this Peaceful Coexistence Coalition of NERDS and the Thunder of Allah and his followers felt a mutual dependence on this one great miracle.

When the Thunder of Allah returned to the Mideast, he gathered his own group of scholars and sales people and Internet specialists and social media gurus, and they began a campaign of lectures and meeting and slideshows and blogs and tracts and pamphlets with a nearly religious fervor. Gradually and increasingly, the Miracle unfolded. And as it unfolded, it felt like the winding down of a fine timepiece, and even the dismantling of a bomb (literally).

The facts spoke for themselves, but the Thunder of Allah's masterful team of scholars and sales people and Internet specialists and social media gurus also spoke for them.

And then, like John F. Kennedy's Peace Corp and VISTA in the 1960's, a volunteer group movement picked up traction. Volunteers from the United Arab Emirates were joined by Egyptian volunteers and Saudi Arabian volunteers and Syrian volunteers and Iraqi volunteers and Iranian volunteers and Jordanian volunteers who all mistrusted the West but who unanimously believed that—for this brief and important moment in time—the problem at hand could be solved by a concerted group effort and that a cataclysmic war could be averted, at least for now.

The Mideast Volunteers were joined by Volunteers from around the world, and they gathered on the Eastern shores of the Mediterranean Sea, the Northern shores of the Red Sea, and the Northern shores of the Persian Gulf near the point where the Tigris and Euphrates Rivers joined together and flowed into the Gulf.

And foundations and governments and private industry pitched in to help the volunteer effort. Several foundations offered grants to cover the costs of travel and food and lodging for the volunteers. National and regional governments offered engineering and technical expertise to guide the volunteers on their project. And private industry—even the Frackers themselves—generously donated time and equipment to assure that the project would be completed as safely and efficiently as possible.

The fracking drills were put into action; the absorbent Super Hybrid Sponges were laid into place; the deep and powerful Super Hybrid Bamboo Fig roots were planted; and the sea water was directed to strategic volcanic centers hundred of miles away where it was vaporized and boiled and sent by steam pressure to the surface to form miraculous Artesian Springs like Al Ain.

The scientific reality of a possible world end through pollution, overpopulation and/or cataclysmic war was counter punched by the scientific reality of clean, pure and plentiful water for everyone on Earth, and at least a temporary state of Peaceful Coexistence. It was beautiful, it was miraculous, it was **FRACKING BRILLIANT!**

www.ingramcontent.com/pod-product-compliance
Lightning Source LLC
Chambersburg PA
CBHW030815170726
47995CB00013B/974